CoComelon™

HIDE-AND-SEEK FUN!

Adapted by Maria Le
Ready-to-Read

SIMON SPOTLIGHT

An imprint of Simon & Schuster Children's Publishing Division • New York London Toronto Sydney New Delhi
1230 Avenue of the Americas, New York, New York 10020 • This Simon Spotlight edition August 2024
CoComelon™ & © 2024 Moonbug Entertainment. All Rights Reserved. • All rights reserved, including
the right of reproduction in whole or in part in any form. • SIMON SPOTLIGHT, READY-TO-READ, and
colophon are registered trademarks of Simon & Schuster, LLC. • Simon & Schuster: Celebrating 100 Years
of Publishing in 2024 • For information about special discounts for bulk purchases, please contact
Simon & Schuster Special Sales at 1-866-506-1949 or business@simonandschuster.com.
Manufactured in the United States of America 0724 LAK • 10 9 8 7 6 5 4 3 2 1
ISBN 978-1-6659-6035-9 (hc) • ISBN 978-1-6659-6034-2 (pbk) • ISBN 978-1-6659-6036-6 (ebook)

Here is a list of all the words you will find in this book. Sound them out before you begin reading the story.

Names:

 Cece

 Cody

 JJ

 Mateo

 Nina

Word families:

"-eek" $\longrightarrow$ p**eek** s**eek**

Sight words:

and	his	is	not	one
play	three	two	where	will
you				

Bonus words:

finds	friends	hide	peek
seek			

Ready to go? Happy reading!

Don't miss the questions about the story
on the last page of this book.

JJ and his friends play hide-and-seek.

JJ will not peek.

Three, two, one!
JJ will seek!

JJ finds Nina and Mateo!

JJ finds Cody!

JJ finds Cece!

Cece will not peek.

Three, two, one!
Cece will seek!

Nina and Mateo hide.

Cece finds
Nina and Mateo!

Cody will not peek.

Three, two, one!
Cody will seek!

Nina and Mateo
hide.

Cody finds Nina and Mateo!

Nina will not peek.

Three, two, one!
Nina will seek.

Nina finds Cece!

Nina finds Cody!

Nina finds JJ!

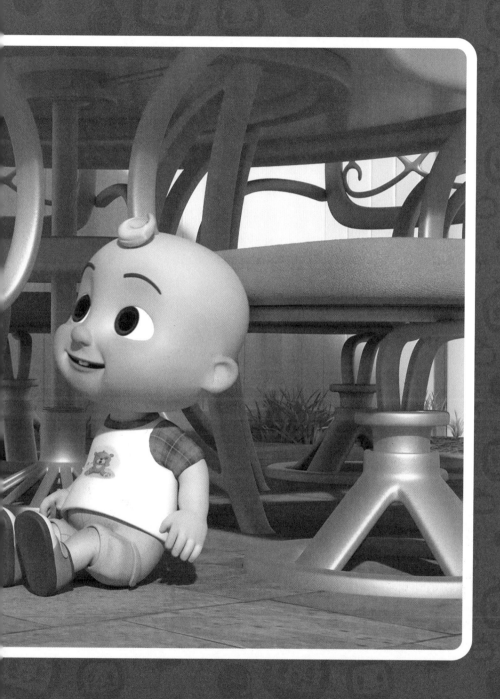

Where is Mateo?

Nina will seek!

Nina finds Mateo!

Will you play
hide-and-seek?

Now that you have read the story, can you answer these questions?

1. Who seeks at the beginning of the story? Who seeks at the end of the story?

2. Where does Nina find Mateo?

3. In this story you read the words "seek" and "peek." Those words rhyme. Can you think of other words that rhyme with "seek" and "peek"?

Great job! You are a reading star!